TIME-AGO LOST
More Tales of Jahdu

TIME-AGO

BY VIRGINIA HAMILTON

ILLUSTRATED BY RAY PRATHER

LOST More Tales of Jahdu

The Macmillan Company, New York, New York ✓

The Macmillan Company, 866 Third Avenue, New York, N.Y. 10022
Collier-Macmillan Canada Ltd., Toronto, Ontario

Library of Congress catalog card number: 72–85187

Printed in the United States of America

1 2 3 4 5 6 7 8 9 10

For Elizabeth English,
Jaime, Leigh,
and Susan

Contents

1.

How Jahdu Ran Through Darkness in No Time at All

MAMA LUKA sat in her tight little room in a fine, good place called Harlem. She sat facing the window with her chin resting in the palm of her hand. Yes, she did. The window blinds were raised high to let in the rays of the sun. But there was no sunlight this day, for rain poured down the window in a steady stream.

Mama Luka watched over Lee Edward while his mother worked and while his father found work whenever he could. Lee Edward came to her house as soon as his school was out for the day. He came, smiling and laughing, because he loved the Jahdu stories Mama Luka would tell. He loved the way she would reach into the air to catch a Jahdu story going by. He loved Mama Luka almost as much as he loved his own mama. Mama Luka sometimes called him Little Brother the way his own mama did. But this day, Mama Luka had been quiet more than once.

"If this rain won't stop its crying," she told Lee Edward, "I'm going to bed for a month of Sundays."

Lee Edward sat close to Mama Luka where he liked to be. He could see the way she smiled and hear every word she said. But Mama Luka wouldn't smile. She wouldn't talk much and Lee Edward didn't know how to make her feel good again. He didn't know how to shut off the rain. Now claps of thunder rolled around the sky, filling Mama Luka's room with loudness, like anger.

Mama Luka had a letter beside her. Once and again she read the letter and then placed it next to her on the chair. Every time she did that, Lee Edward tried hard to find something to say.

"Mama Luka, I like your hair like that," he told her. "It's the best beautiful hair I ever did see."

"Little Brother, thank you so much," she said. She had to smile. "Do you really like my hair like this?"

"I like the way it is long and the way it is black," Lee Edward said.

"So do I," said Mama Luka. "I never will cut it."

"No, never do," said Lee Edward.

"I never will sell it to the people who make wigs, either," Mama Luka said.

"Never do," Lee Edward said again.

Mama Luka had black skin and a nose as curved as the beak of a parrot. She could wear her hair in one long pigtail down her back and she could sit on it. But now she had un-braided her hair so it fell over her shoulders. It hung down her back in waves of dark.

There was a rumble of thunder. The rain hit Mama Luka's window harder, like it meant to come straight through.

Lee Edward shivered. "Look's like the sun's never coming out again," he said. "Wouldn't it be something if it never did?"

"Be something I surely wouldn't like," Mama Luka told him, "but you know, once it did rain forty days and forty nights."

Lee Edward grinned. "That was in Noah's time," he said, "but the sun did come out again after the flood."

"And that's the truth," said Mama Luka. "Yet, I remember me a time . . . a Jahdu time. . . ."

Lee Edward stared at Mama Luka. She had reached into the air to grab something Lee Edward couldn't see. Whatever Mama Luka had taken out of the air must have been dark and wiggly. She had to open her eyes wide to see it. And she had a time keeping it quiet in her lap.

Lee Edward was happy. Even with the thunder rolling around and banging against the sky, and even with the rain hitting the window in a steady fall, and even with the letter which had first made Mama Luka feel blue, she was still going to tell a Jahdu tale.

"Goody for me!" Lee Edward yelled. "Mama Luka, what one is it?"

"Slow down there, you darkness thing," Mama Luka said to what Lee Edward couldn't see. She cupped her hands over her mouth and swallowed what had been in her hands.

"A darkness thing?" said Lee Edward. "How does it taste?"

But Mama Luka wouldn't say. She never would tell anything before she was ready. She knew a roomful of Jahdu stories. She knew what Jahdu looked like, but that was her secret. She always knew where he had been and where he was going. She told every Jahdu story slow and easy, just the way she was about to tell one now.

"Lee Edward," she began, "I can't find me one taste in this story that lasts long enough for me to tell you about it."

"Well, tell me *something*," Lee Edward said.

"I can tell you this," Mama Luka said. "We have here a Jahdu story of a time-ago lost."

"A what kind of time?" Lee Edward wanted to know.

Mama Luka looked closely at Lee Edward. "Little Brother, are you going to be scared?" she asked him.

"Maybe a little," he said. "I don't like darkness things so much."

"You still want me to tell you about it?" asked Mama Luka.

"I don't care if it is scary!" Lee Edward finally said.

"Darkness won't have to mean scary," said Mama Luka.

"So tell it," Lee Edward said.

"I'm getting myself ready," said Mama Luka.

THIS IS THE JAHDU STORY SO DARK AND WIGGLY,
ABOUT A TIME-AGO LOST,
THAT MAMA LUKA TOLD TO LEE EDWARD.

Jahdu came running along. He was heading east to the place where he had been born, for he thought he had better be born again. Yes, he did. He was running out of his Jahdu dust that put things to sleep and woke them up. And he would have to be reborn in order to get enough Jahdu dust.

Jahdu had been to the good place called Harlem. He had been a strong black boy who owned a dog named Rufus. But Jahdu never stayed one kind of person for very long. He had learned how to change himself into whomever he wished from his friend Chameleon. Now he was his own Jahdu self again.

"Woogily!" said Jahdu after a long time of running. "The East surely is far and far. It has been night longer than any night I can remember. I wish it would end and morning would come."

Jahdu kept running on. He couldn't see a thing on either side of him. He couldn't see where he had been or where he was going through the darkness. Jahdu should have walked instead of running but he had not been in the world forever. Even though he could turn himself into whatever he wished, and even though he had magic enough to put things to sleep and wake them up again, he was still very young. And he was only three and one-half feet tall.

All at once, Jahdu tripped over something and fell, sprawled on the ground.

"Now what was that lying right in the middle of the dark?" Jahdu said.

"A-heh, a-heh-heh," a voice went, laughing.

"Who in the world is that?" Jahdu said to the darkness.

"How you was, Jahdu?" said the voice. "A-heh, a-heh-heh."

Jahdu felt around on the ground. He felt a short tuft of something, like a feathery tail. He felt some flat toes grown together and another something the same, like a pair of webbed feet. Jahdu caught hold of a large, feathered body lying on its back. He touched a queer bird's head with a bill pointing straight up in the darkness. From head to foot, the big crazy bird smelled like fish.

"Phew!" said Jahdu.

"Loon-a-tic," said the bird, "loon-a-tock. Wind my fish and eat my clock."

"You crazy, Loon," Jahdu said. "What are you doing lying on the ground?" He knew his old friend Loon, even in the dark. But never before had he heard of Loon lying on his back.

Lazily, Loon said, "How you doing, Jahdu?"

"I'm doing fine," said Jahdu, "but why aren't you flying over some ocean searching for your supper?"

"I haven't got the time," Loon said, very carefully. "Have you got the time, Jahdu?"

"Now why would I want to go flying over water in search of my supper?" asked Jahdu.

"Have you . . ." Loon began, sounding nervous, "got the time?"

"What's the matter with you?" Jahdu said. "And no, I haven't got the time. All I know is that it's night and it's been the longest night I've ever run through."

"That's what I thinking," Loon said excitedly.

"You're not making much sense," Jahdu told him. "Here, let me help you up."

"I staying right laying low," said Loon. "A-heh, a-heh-heh."

Lying out here in the dark, Jahdu thought, I bet old Loon caught himself some kind of head cold.

"Loon," he said, "how long have you been stretched out on your back?"

"A-heh," Loon said, shaking all over. "Go ask time, I haven't got the anybody."

"What are you trying to say?" Jahdu asked.

"Just going right, keep on," said crazy Loon. "Light gets until it."

"What in the world!" Jahdu said, holding onto Loon as tightly as he could.

"Light way all the not," said Loon. And then, shouting, "GRAY BUT SOMEWHAT!"

"Poor Loon," said Jahdu. "You were always silly. But now you are really scared and I can't make head nor tail out of what you're saying." Jahdu smoothed out Loon's long feathers. "You were my friend," he said. "Remember the time I used my magic to put you to sleep? Then I woke you up and you took off flying over the ocean looking for me. It wasn't until you spotted me and were about to land that you found out your feet were tied together. Remember that trick I played, Loon?"

"A-heh, yeah," Loon said, calmer now.

"You had to crash-land," Jahdu went on. "Your head was

buried a foot deep in the sand when I found you—you're not still mad at me, are you, Loon?"

Loon was quiet a moment. "A-heh, no, Jahdu," he said at last. "Just find me some light."

"Find your own light," said Jahdu. "I just remembered, I have to be running along."

"But it gone," Loon said. "All light gone and I lost in the dark."

Loon sounded so pitiful that Jahdu couldn't very well leave him.

"Oh, all right, you can ride with me," Jahdu told him. "Here, climb up and hold on tight."

Jahdu strained under Loon's weight, then steadied himself. "Now you lead the way," he told Loon. "Just sniff for fish wherever there might be fish. Once you smell fish, we have found water and you can eat. I wouldn't mind having a few fish myself to help me along to the East."

So Jahdu and Loon went running on. That is, Jahdu went running and Loon went on riding. After a long time of riding and running, in which darkness stayed dark and light was nowhere to be seen, Loon moved his bill to the right of Jahdu.

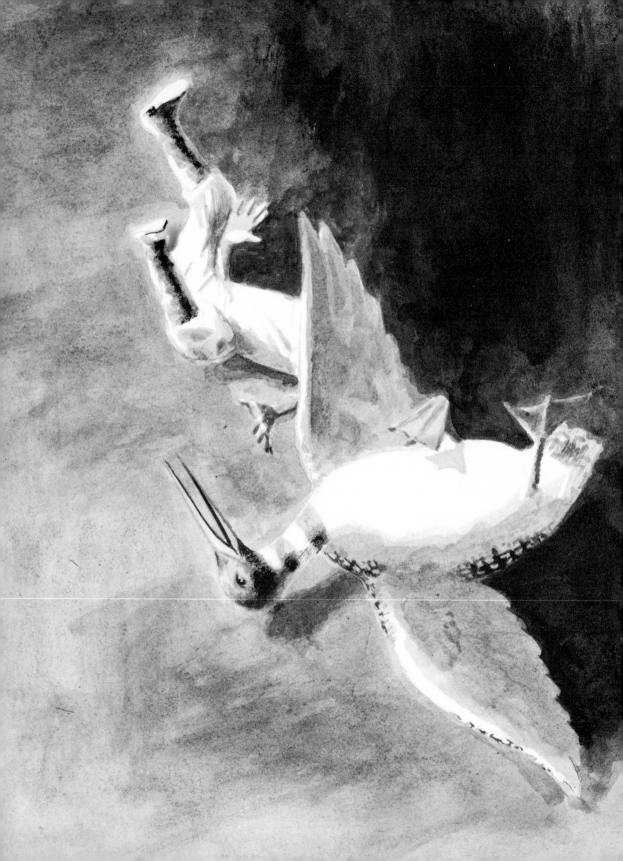

"You want me to go south?" Jahdu asked him.

"A-heh, yes," Loon said.

Jahdu veered to the right for what seemed nights. Then, with another nudge from the bill of Loon, he went east again. After a long panting silence of running, Jahdu yelled out through the dark: "I can smell it! Loon, there is salt in the air!"

Jahdu smelled the salt of seawater but Loon was smelling fish of seawater. He was smelling fish and more fish and so much fish, he tried to fly away from Jahdu right then and there.

"Stay where you are," Jahdu told him. "We'll be there pretty soon. But looky here, have you noticed something? I can almost see in front of me. I mean, I think I can almost see. It's getting lighter, or at least, not quite so dark. Doesn't that make you feel better, Loon? Loon . . . ?"

Loon was still swooning over the smell of fish. He was numb and deaf because of the sweet smell of fish.

"It's all right, poor old Loon. We're almost there now," Jahdu told him. "I can hear water lapping at the seashore."

All at once Jahdu bumped into something and bounced away from it. Jahdu lost his balance and he and Loon rolled down what felt like a low, sandy hill. With a great splash, he and Loon tumbled into chilly water full of the most juicy fish Loon ever did gobble up as fast as he could.

Jahdu had never eaten raw fish. But he swallowed them now so that he could run that much faster to the East.

"Woogily!" he said. "That was the most sudden surprise I've had in this darkness." Jahdu sat still and looked around as hard as he could. "I can see things," he said. "I can almost see shadow. There's almost a shadow up there on the sand bank. And the shadow is . . . almost . . . fishing!"

The almost shadow sat comfortably, as if he were sitting in the sun.

"Well, for goodness sake," said Jahdu, going closer to the almost shadow, "good evening, friend Fisherman, I think Loon and I must have tripped over you."

Fisherman didn't say anything. He kept right on doing what he had been doing, which was almost fishing. When Jahdu peered through the dark and gazed at the shadow, he saw that Fisherman wasn't fishing at all.

"Friend Fisherman," Jahdu said, "you've got your fishhook stuck in the sand."

Fisherman went on reeling in his line with a few grains of

sand covering his fishhook and emptying the bit of sand into his fish box. Yes, he did.

"Something is awfully wrong with this fisherman," Jahdu said to himself. "If I could just light up this place a little."

"Pardon me," Jahdu said to Fisherman. "Would you happen to have a match on you? That's too bad," Jahdu added when Fisherman didn't answer.

Jahdu peered into Fisherman's face. He couldn't see much, even up close. Far off in the water he could hear Loon still busy catching fish.

"Fisherman," said Jahdu, "you could catch fish just like Loon out there. All you have to do is ease yourself toward the water's edge. Then you could cast your rod into the water and catch all kinds of fish. Well, Fisherman, did you hear me? Fisherman!"

"Haven't got the time," Fisherman finally said, very sadly. He reeled in his line and emptied the few grains of sand into his fish box.

"You're as crazy as Loon," Jahdu told him, "but *you* make me angry!" With that, Jahdu began running around Fisherman as fast as he could. Faster and faster he ran as only Jahdu knew how.

As soon as the Jahdu dust fell, Fisherman should have fallen asleep. But he didn't, for Jahdu's dust was not as strong as it used to be.

"Woogily!" said Jahdu. "I'd better give Fisherman some more of my dust." He ran around Fisherman a second time. More Jahdu dust rose out of Jahdu and fell over Fisherman. And this time Fisherman fell fast asleep.

"There!" said Jahdu. "I still have my magic but I'd better get to the East and be reborn before it's all gone."

Just then old Loon came waddling out of the water. His bill bulged with the fish he'd already eaten.

"How can you be so piggish?" Jahdu said to him. "I think you'd better empty your bill of fish into Fisherman's fish box."

In the shadowy dark, Loon shook his head.

"I put that fisherman to sleep for fishing in the sand," said Jahdu. "If you're not careful, I'll put you to sleep as well. And you'll stay asleep until I decide to wake you up again."

Suddenly Loon took a flying leap straight up in the air. But try as he might for a quick take-off, he'd eaten too many fish. He couldn't get his fat belly off the ground.

"Serves you right," Jahdu told him. "You'd better not try a stunt like that again."

16

Jahdu led Loon over to the fisherman's fish box. He tickled Loon under his right wing where he was most ticklish. Loon laughed so hard, fish flew out of his bill into Fisherman's fish box.

"A-heh! Whoo-hoo! Ahhhh-a-haaa!" Loon sighed.

"Well, of course you feel better," Jahdu told him. "No Loon could even swallow with that many fish in his bill. Now. You listen to me. I want you to stay right here with Fisherman until I . . ."

Jahdu never had a chance to finish what he had started to say. For all at once Loon ran to the water. Whistling like Loons will do and flapping his wings in a fury, he made clouds of sand-dust darkness. Yes, he did. He skimmed over the water, skating along on his webbed toes. But his wings tired out and he sank like a stone, straight to the bottom.

Jahdu had to dive in and haul him out. "Loon, you dumb bird!" Jahdu said. "I ought to . . . I really ought—I think I will." He hurled big, soggy Loon onto the sand and began running around him fast and faster. A tiny bit of Jahdu dust rose out of Jahdu and fell over Loon. It was only enough dust to make Loon yawn twice.

"Oh, my goodness," said Jahdu. He had to run around

Loon three times. Loon tried to get away each time.

"Stand still, Loon," Jahdu yelled.

"Won't," said Loon, and he didn't.

But finally, Jahdu was able to run around Loon in circles. When all that was left of the Jahdu dust settled, Loon was deeply asleep and snoring his loonful tune.

Jahdu stayed close by Fisherman and the snoring Loon. During one long period of quiet snoring Loon commenced talking in his sleep and Fisherman began walking.

"What a silly pair," Jahdu said. "I should let them sleep for a whole night year. I would, too, if I didn't have to be hurrying on."

Jahdu started running around Loon and Fisherman slowly and slower. What little Jahdu dust there was rose out of Fisherman and Loon and settled back into Jahdu. Very quickly, Loon and Fisherman gave every sign of waking. When they were sleepily sitting, Jahdu spoke to them.

"I've got to be going," he said to both of them. "Loon here can catch you some fish," he told Fisherman.

"Jahdu, don't leave me here in the dark," Loon said, sounding ready to cry.

"I have to," Jahdu said. "You saw how little dust I have

left. I've got to get to the East as fast as I can to get me
some more dust."

"Take me with you," Loon said mournfully.

"I can't carry you all that way, Loon, I'm sorry," Jahdu
told him.

"But it dark!" Loon cried. "I lost. I scared."

"I know!" said Jahdu, patting Loon's feathers. "And it's
a strange, long kind of dark. Do you remember when it
started?"

"No," said Loon. "I only afraid. I only out of food. I
only could think of being scared and hungry."

"Well, I didn't pay much attention to the dark either,"
said Jahdu. "When you have magic the way I do, you don't
bother about the length of a night."

Jahdu and Loon were silent. After a while, they thought to
move Fisherman close to the water's edge so he could catch
his own fish.

"See?" Loon said. "He be all right. Take me with you."

"Loon, I told you, I've got to travel fast to the East. You're
too slow to walk and you can't see to fly, which means I'd
have to carry you. But listen, I'll help you out if I can."

"How, Jahdu?" asked Loon.

"Just for you," Jahdu said grandly, "I'll find out what's happened to the light."

"Just for me?" said Loon.

"You're my friend, aren't you?" said Jahdu.

"And will be ever, Jahdu," said Loon.

"Then it's settled," Jahdu told him. "You stay right here where you have as much fish as you want."

Loon began to look doubtful, and Jahdu said quickly, "A little while ago when you were sleeping, I heard this lion roaring in the dark. He sure did sound hungry!"

"A-heh-heh," Loon said, "I guess I stay put. No telling what going to wander out there in darkness."

"So good-by, old Loon," Jahdu said. Already, he was running away. "Good-by, Fisherman," he called. "I hope to see you both after I've found the East . . . and what's happened to the light, too."

"Good-by, a-heh, Jahdu," Loon called sadly.

Jahdu went running on. He had what was left of his Jahdu magic back within him. He was alone again in darkness and he was glad to be on his way. The darkness did have some shadow now. Jahdu followed the shadow dark toward the East.

20

"Woogily!" Jahdu said. "I'm so glad to be running along again. I'm going to be reborn. It can just stay dark forever, I don't care!"

THIS IS THE END OF THE JAHDU STORY SO WIGGLY AND DARK,
OF A TIME-AGO LOST,
THAT MAMA LUKA TOLD ONE DAY TO LEE EDWARD.

2.
How Jahdu Found a Fire to Light His Way

MAMA LUKA stared out of her window and hummed a toneless tune. The rain had stopped for a while. But there was still thunder rumbling and the promise of more rain.

"Is that all?" Lee Edward said, when it seemed as if Mama Luka had finished the Jahdu tale of Loon and Fisherman.

22

"That certainly is all of that story," Mama Luka told him.

Lee Edward thought for a minute. Then he said, "Jahdu is just bad-tempered and mean! He told the loon he'd find out what happened to the light. But he won't, I know he won't."

"Now, now," Mama Luka said soothingly. She took a jar of red licorice off the table and handed Lee Edward a long licorice twist. "Jahdu had been running through that darkness for what seemed like forever," she said, "and he was getting pretty tired."

"Well . . ." Lee Edward began, "maybe he was just getting cranky. I know I get cranky when I'm tired."

"That's the truth," said Mama Luka. "He surely was cranky. But he did carry old Loon for a long way, now didn't he?"

"Yes," said Lee Edward.

"And he did make sure the fisherman had some fish and that Loon didn't go off by himself in the dark."

"But he lied about the lion," Lee Edward said.

"Just a little lie," Mama Luka said. "Jahdu wasn't scared of the dark but Loon was. And being scared, Loon could hurt himself."

Lee Edward's face broke into a smile. "Jahdu didn't want

to be bothered with Loon or anybody, but he wasn't being mean."

"That's right," said Mama Luka. "Jahdu was, well, just Jahduing his way to the East. He was in an awful hurry to be reborn and he just might find out what happened to the light on his way.

"You'll recall," Mama Luka went on, "that Jahdu had been hard to handle ever since he outsmarted the giant, Trouble. You remember that big old Trouble, don't you, Lee Edward?"

"I remember that story," Lee Edward said. "Sure, and Jahdu thought he was smarter than anybody."

"That's right," Mama Luka said.

"Did Jahdu ever meet up with Trouble again?" Lee Edward asked.

"I'm sure he must have," Mama Luka said, "but you've got to find the story. I took over your job when I picked that last story out of the air for you."

"I didn't even notice you picked it," Lee Edward said.

"I'm sorry for picking it," Mama Luka told him, "and just to show you, I'll let you pick another one."

"You mean today?" Mama Luka always did tell just one Jahdu story a day.

"Sure. Go on and pick it," said Mama Luka, "a Trouble one, a darkness one—any kind you like." She leaned forward so she could tell for sure what kind of story Lee Edward wanted.

"I think I'll pick a little bit of both," Lee Edward said. "I think I'll pick . . . that one!" He pointed to a space at the tip of Mama Luka's curved nose.

Mama Luka grabbed the space—smack!—right between her palms. She almost caught the tip of her nose, too. She stretched her arms out in front of her face, as though she was about to catch a ball. Suddenly her hands began to tremble. "Ooooh, Little Brother!" she said.

"What is it?" Lee Edward whispered, his eyes wide as they could be.

"Lordy, this is some kind of Jahdu story!" Mama Luka told him. "I've never held one so strong or so hot to handle."

"Mama Luka, are you going to taste it?"

"I wouldn't dare taste it," she said. "It might burn my mouth."

"Then tell it!" Lee Edward said.

"Here it comes," said Mama Luka.

26

THIS IS THE JAHDU STORY
SO STRONG AND HOT TO HANDLE
THAT MAMA LUKA TOLD TO LEE EDWARD.

Jahdu was running on and on. He was running through darkness with shadow just ahead of him. It was a long time before Jahdu realized that the shadow was running, too.

"Now wait a minute," Jahdu said to himself. "How is it my shadow is here when there is no light?"

Suddenly the shadow up ahead stopped its running. When Jahdu caught up with it, the shadow started running alongside Jahdu, scaring Jahdu half to death.

Jahdu leaped high in the air out of fear. "Woogily!" he said on the way down.

"How you doing, Jahdu?" said Shadow, as they began running again.

"I'm doing all right," Jahdu told him, "but I never did talk to my shadow before. I never did cast a shadow where there is no light at all."

"Oh, well," said Shadow, "you have to understand. I'm not just your shadow and maybe that's why I can talk and kind of move about on my own. You see, I'm everybody's

27

shadow come together as long as there is no light."

"How long hasn't there been light?" Jahdu asked. "I have a friend who is afraid of so much darkness."

"I don't know too much about it," Shadow said, "but I do know that times have changed. There won't be light anymore, I figure. Because it's been this kind of dark for so long, it must be going to be dark forever."

"Oh, no," said Jahdu, "I don't believe that."

"Why don't you believe it?" asked Shadow. "Didn't I just tell you? I'm a part of you, so I've got to be telling the truth."

"It's true you're a part of me," Jahdu said, "but from what you say, you're a part of everybody, too."

"You trying to tell me everybody is lying?"

"I'm not trying to tell you anything," Jahdu said. "I'm just saying I can't believe it's going to be dark forever."

"No?" said Shadow.

"No," said Jahdu.

"All right, then," said Shadow, and he was gone.

Jahdu was plunged into darkness with no Shadow anywhere. He had been running fast while there was Shadow but now he had the good sense to slow down.

"How do you like that, Jahdu?" called a voice from far off.

"You'll never amount to anything!" Jahdu shouted through the darkness. "Shadow, you'll never have anybody!"

"Maybe not," called back Shadow, "but you're out there all by yourself with nothing to guide you."

"I never needed you to guide me anywhere!" Jahdu yelled.

"No?" called Shadow. "Then why are you heading west?"

Jahdu stopped dead in his tracks. Everything was black around him and awfully quiet.

"Woogily!" said Jahdu. "I let that shadow trick me, I surely did.

"Hey!" Jahdu called out. "That was a good trick, but how about heading me toward the East again?"

"Sorry, Jahdu," called Shadow from way far away. "You're on your own. But I'll tell you one thing, before you find the East, you're in for a big shock."

Softly, Jahdu called, "Shadow?" But the shadow would not answer again.

Jahdu felt almost afraid. Yes, he did. "I don't know which way to go," he said to himself. "I've got to hurry and I'm going to go and go until I find something to show me I'm going east."

So Jahdu hurried off, first north, then south and west. He had no idea which way he went, for all was night. Jahdu ran for nights and nights. Every now and again he stumbled over a small animal or bird. Once he tripped over a farmer but the farmer made no sense at all.

"I haven't got a minute to waste," the farmer had said to Jahdu. Yet the farmer made no move to go. He lay there in the darkness as if he had all the time in the world.

Soon Jahdu left the farmer far behind, or ahead, he couldn't tell which in all that dark. He was alone for a long, empty time until one night the earth trembled and the darkness throbbed in huge, moving spaces. There was sound: "Ga-roammm, ga-roammm." Then it came louder: "GA-ROAMMM, GA-ROAMMM." It was so piercing that Jahdu stopped dead in the dark.

"Who . . . who is it, please?" Jahdu called through the night.

"How you doing, stranger?" said so many loud voices from on high.

At once, Jahdu knew who spoke. It was a herd of great, woolly mammoths moving across the earth.

"Hey, wait!" Jahdu called, "I remember you from a long

time ago. Wait for me! Where are you going—are you heading east?"

"Ga-roammm, ga-roammm," called the mammoths from a long way off. Once mammoths got going, they had to keep going, they were so large.

"Can't stop, little stranger," they called, "for we haven't got the time."

"Just tell me if you are heading east!" Jahdu yelled after them.

"Ga-roam-roammm, ga-roammm," was all the mammoths said before the earth settled down again and they were gone.

Now what are mammoths doing here when mammoths lived so very long ago? Jahdu wondered.

He kept on running and he kept thinking about the mammoths.

"They lived at the beginning of time," he said as he ran. "The first sun rose . . . the first light came . . . mammoths lived . . . as time began! Oh, of course! I must be close to the East. And the closer I come to it, the farther back in time I go."

Jahdu ran and ran. In what direction he ran he wasn't sure, but he thought he was heading east. It was not long before he saw something through the darkness. Soon he was sure he was seeing something other than night.

"Woogily!" said Jahdu. "The darkness up ahead is up and up, high upon itself. It's piled up just like . . . mountains!"

Swiftly, Jahdu ran to the mountains, for he was seeing them almost clearly now. By the time he reached the top of one low mountain, he knew he had found a whole mountain range.

"Woogily!" said Jahdu. "This is some high place with more than fifty-two mountains that I can see."

He looked all around and for the first time he noticed that the mountains lay deep in shadow.

"Oh, my goodness!" he said, as the mountains heaved and shook in rhythm with the shadow that rose and fell. Jahdu tried running down the low mountain as fast as he could. Before he could get away, the great giant, Trouble, had him cupped snugly in his strong left hand.

"How you doing, Trouble?" said Jahdu quietly. "I never thought I'd run into you out here in all this darkness."

"But I told you you were in for a big shock," said Shadow, lying quietly on one side of the giant.

"How are you, little friend?" said Trouble. "And who might you be?"

"You mean to say you don't remember Jahdu, who is always running along?" asked Jahdu.

"I know a friend when I see one," said Trouble, "but I don't think I've come across one called Jahdu."

"Strange," said Jahdu. "I came across you once, a long time ago."

"Time-ago?" said Trouble. "There's no time-ago that I know of. There is only here and now."

"Oh, I see. I think I do see," said Jahdu, "but never mind about that. Tell me something. Do you still have your earring which is made from a barrel?" Jahdu remembered that the barrel of Trouble was as large as a water tower.

"Well, sure I have my barrel," said Trouble, "but how did you know about that, little Jahdu? I only found it a few nights ago before I lay me down to rest."

"And there are no people in your barrel of an earring?" asked Jahdu, very interested.

"There are no people in it," said Trouble. "There's just a bit of rainwater down at the bottom."

"Let me get this straight," said Jahdu. "You don't want to put me in your barrel?"

"No," said Trouble. "In fact, I grew tired of having that barrel dangling from my earlobe. I took it off and put it over there in the deep shadow."

Sure enough, Jahdu saw the barrel lying on its side, with rainwater dripping out of it.

"Listen, Trouble," said Jahdu, "do you have any idea where the East is? I've asked everybody all through the darkness and nobody will tell me. Everybody keeps saying they haven't got the time."

"The East lies just over my right shoulder," said Trouble. "And what is this all about time, anyway?"

"Would you hold me up a little higher," Jahdu said quickly, "so I can see the East?"

"Take a look as long as you like," Trouble told him.

Cupped in Trouble's hand, Jahdu looked over Trouble's right shoulder. At the far edge of darkness, way far away, he saw a pale color.

"Woogily!" yelled Jahdu. Yes, he did. "There it is!" he said. "Way out there is the East, just the place I've been looking for. And way out there is something dim."

I can be reborn, Jahdu thought. And if that pale color is the light, then I have found it without even trying.

"Trouble," Jahdu said suddenly, "out there is the only

pale color I've seen in all of this darkness."

"Of course, little friend," said the giant. "There is color in the East and it is the only color I know of."

"That's why no one had the time!" said Jahdu.

"What?" said Trouble.

"Once there was plenty of light," said Jahdu, "and once there was plenty of time. But I think now something is holding the light in the East. It is keeping back the time, also. That's why we have so little of either and why there is only darkness."

"What are you talking about, little Jahdu?" Trouble said kindly.

"Oh, nothing at all," Jahdu told him. "By the way, you wouldn't happen to have a match on you, would you, Trouble? I'd like to be able to see my way to the East and I'd like to be running as fast as I can run."

Trouble was silent, but Shadow spoke up: "In your shirt pocket," said the shadow.

"Oh, you mean these," Trouble said, patting his pocket.

"Do you think you could lend me a match?" asked Jahdu.

"Sure," Trouble said. "I've got plenty of—what do you call them—matches."

"And . . . and . . ." Jahdu stammered, "would you mind

lighting it for me? Just whisk it along your pants leg very fast."

"All right," said the giant.

Trouble fumbled in his shirt pocket. He brought out a match the size of a tall pine tree. Then he whisked the match along his trousers. There was a burst of yellow light the size of a house on fire. "Woogily!" shouted Jahdu.

"Hardly light enough to see by," said Trouble.

"Maybe not for your giant eyes," Jahdu told him, "but for me, it is a great light.

"Now, Trouble," said Jahdu, "I wish to ask another favor."

"Anything at all," the giant said.

Jahdu couldn't quite believe that Trouble was really nice. He remembered how Trouble used to put people and babies and lions and donkeys in his barrel and keep them there. Just as mean as any giant ever could be.

He's forgotten every bit of it, Jahdu thought, because the closer you come to the East, the less you remember. Something is keeping back the time and the light. And something is keeping Trouble's memory from him.

"Would you mind putting your barrel over there near the East?" Jahdu asked the giant.

"I don't mind," said Trouble.

"And would you mind lighting it before your match goes out?"

"I don't mind," Trouble said again. He picked up the empty barrel and flicked it over his right shoulder. With a crash, it landed in darkness near the East.

"And would you sit me down over there in the darkness, about a half a mile from your barrel?"

"If that's what you want," said Trouble, and he did as Jahdu asked.

"NOW, GIANT TROUBLE," Jahdu shouted, "LIGHT THE BARREL."

Trouble chuckled a sound like a waterfall. "All right," he said.

There was a burst of burning light like a forest on fire. Through the firelight, Jahdu ran to the East as fast as he could. He could hear behind him the shadow sighing. Jahdu thought to glance back. He couldn't see the shadow at all. Shadow had been swallowed up by the firelight and was sleeping for as long as the firelight burned.

Jahdu could see Trouble. Yes, he could. The burning barrel made light. Yes, it did. Trouble could see Jahdu and Trouble could remember for as long as the firelight lasted.

The earth shook as Trouble stood to his giant height. His

face was rain-cloud dark and full of stormy anger. His feet were as big as steamships. His legs were as long as highways.

Jahdu ran and ran. The great right hand of Trouble swooped down and just missed catching him.

"Woogily!" said Jahdu, glancing over his shoulder. He saw that Trouble's left hand was already packed full of donkeys and birds and even some people. They were wandering around in the darkness and had been caught by Trouble once there was firelight.

"Jahdu!" cried Trouble in a voice like the roar of a hurricane.

Jahdu kept running on and on. The last thing he heard Trouble say was: "My barrel. You made me burn my barrel. Now where is Trouble to keep his friends?"

"You have to let them go," Jahdu yelled, not caring if Trouble heard him. "I outsmarted you again, you big old Trouble. You'll have to let all your friends run along like me!"

As soon as the false light of the barrel began to fade, Trouble started losing his memory again. He was surprised to find monkeys and babies clutched in his palm. He set them gently down in the growing shadow. The light of the barrel flickered and died. Trouble stretched himself out on the ground, looking as long and as dark as a whole mountain range.

That is how Jahdu found firelight to see his way quickly to the East, and how he ran into Trouble for the second time.

THIS IS THE END OF THE JAHDU STORY
SO STRONG AND HOT TO HANDLE
THAT MAMA LUKA TOLD TO THE CHILD, LEE EDWARD.

3.
How Jahdu Discovered the Light and Found Enough Time

WINTER had come to the good place called Harlem. Mama Luka cooked spareribs, which she liked better than any other kind of food. She put them in a pan in her oven and then poured sweet-and-sour Chinese sauce over them. The sauce baked deep into the ribs.

This winter day, Mama Luka sat in her room with a plate of sweet-and-sour spareribs before her. Lee Edward was in the room the way he liked to be, right next to Mama Luka's chair. He was seated at a low table eating spareribs covered with Chinese sauce.

"Oh, boy," he said, "these are the best old spareribs I ever tasted."

"And that's the truth," Mama Luka said. "It sure helps make this winter weather feel like spring."

"I'm glad the thunder and lightning are gone," said Lee Edward. It was the day after they had had a terrible rainstorm. "And I'm glad you aren't feeling so blue," Lee Edward added.

Mama Luka had got a letter the day of the rainstorm and the letter had made her feel blue.

"Lee Edward, I'm all right," said Mama Luka. Carefully, she touched the letter she carried in her pocket. But she didn't take it out to read it. "I've seen many a winter come to my street," she said, "and I always feel better when I know Jahdu is out there somewhere just running along."

"Is he?" said Lee Edward.

"Oh, sure," Mama Luka told him. "Why, Jahdu likes

the cold of winter just about as much as he likes the heat of summer."

"He likes running along in the cold?" Lee Edward asked.

"He likes running along in any weather at all," Mama Luka said. "Jahdu just likes running."

"I wonder if he is still running east."

"Maybe so," said Mama Luka.

"And I wonder if he ever did find out what's holding back the light," Lee Edward said.

Mama Luka smiled at Lee Edward and waited.

Lee Edward finished eating the spareribs. So did Mama Luka. He put his plate and Mama Luka's plate in the kitchen sink to one side of Mama Luka's little room. Then he settled down again.

Mama Luka pulled up her window blind to let what light there was enter the room. She had no sooner sat down again than Lee Edward pointed his finger straight up at the ceiling.

Mama Luka reached high up over her head and caught in her hands the space near the ceiling. She swallowed it in one gulp; she shivered and swallowed again.

"How does it taste?" asked Lee Edward.

"Little Brother," Mama Luka said, "that surely was the

best-tasting Jahdu story. It was sweet and sour, just like the Chinese sauce you like so much."

"Then tell it!" Lee Edward said.

"So I'm getting myself ready," Mama Luka answered.

THIS IS THE JAHDU STORY SO SWEET AND SOUR
THAT MAMA LUKA TOLD TO LEE EDWARD.

Jahdu was running along. He had been born once in the East, in an oven next to two loaves of baking bread. One loaf had baked brown and one had baked black but Jahdu hadn't baked at all.

In a grove of elm trees, Jahdu found his old oven again. There were high weeds growing around the oven door. Jahdu had to tramp the weeds down. The oven door creaked and groaned as he opened it.

There were no fresh loaves of bread in Jahdu's old oven. There was just a rusted oven rack which Jahdu climbed upon to be reborn. Carefully, he stretched out on his back to his three and one-half-foot length.

"Woogily!" he said softly, "Jahdu is almost too long for this old oven."

The oven door squeaked and scraped closed. Heat as hot as the sun swirled around Jahdu. The heat was full of dust, for the old oven was dirty. The heat and the dust baked into Jahdu. The heat baked deep but the dust settled in him like sauce on a sparerib.

Ah, that's good, thought Jahdu. Now I will have magic Jahdu dust to last me a long, long time.

Jahdu baked smooth and tender. His shape changed once and then once again. As Jahdu baked, he grew as a boy would grow. And then he slept for a peaceful silence of heat and rest.

Jahdu awoke feeling calm and new. He stretched his young boy's arms. He yawned and climbed out of his old oven. Jahdu bowed deeply to the oven, for now he admired all things that were very old.

Bowing deeply, Jahdu backed his way out of the grove of elm trees. He began running along through a wasteland in the East. West of the wasteland Jahdu saw again the darkness through which he had come.

"Woogily!" said Jahdu, jumping high over a snowbank. He was bundled from head to foot in thick lengths of fur and his ice shoes were caked with snow.

"I'm glad to be a boy of yellow skin and black, black hair," he said. "But this East surely is a cold and frozen land. I haven't seen another boy like me and I wonder where everybody's gone."

Jahdu had a bow and a sheath of arrows slung over his shoulder. Tied to his waist were many small animals which were to be his supper.

Jahdu touched his bow and smiled. I am a bold hunter, he thought. I've been reborn and I might as well help out Loon and everybody. I'll just find out what has happened to the light.

But as Jahdu went running, he found only shade, which covered all of the snow and ice. The sun seemed far deep away from earth and he could find no light anywhere.

"Everything looks so gray," said Jahdu out loud. "I wonder why the sun is not stronger."

"It's the way I like it," said a voice, "and I'm content in all of my days."

Jahdu stopped still in his tracks. He felt fear move up and down his spine.

"Hello," Jahdu said, looking all around.

"How you doing, Jahdu?" said the voice.

"I'm doing fine," said Jahdu, "but how do you know me? Who are you and where are you?"

"I'm Yin, who knows all," said the voice. "I'm the shade all around you."

"Ah, yes," said Jahdu. "You are the shade who lies on the top of things and at the side of things—are you sure you aren't my shadow, too?"

"I'm Yin," said Yin, "who is colored the palest green and gray and white."

"Then you must be the pale color I saw while coming through the darkness," said Jahdu.

"I am," said Yin.

"And you must be the keeper of this long, gray time," Jahdu said.

"I do have my way here," said Yin. "But there's another over there on the boulder."

Slowly Jahdu came near a boulder at the edge of the field of shade. He hadn't seen it, for it blended with a patch of shadeless snow.

"How you doing, Jahdu?" the boulder seemed to say.

"I'm doing all right," said Jahdu, shielding his eyes. The boulder nearly blinded him, it was so bright. "But I've never talked to a boulder before," Jahdu thought to say.

"And you never will," said the voice. "Boulders do not

talk. It's me, Yang, who is speaking. I'm the only warmth and light in all of this land."

"Ah," said Jahdu. "I've been hunting for you! I have a friend who needs you. There is darkness everywhere in the world and my friend is afraid."

"There is darkness because the shade of Yin is powerful here now," said Yang. "Thunder is Yin's friend who holds the clouds together. I am allowed to light only this boulder."

Suddenly Thunder burst overhead with a boom that shook the heavens and even the earth.

"Woogily!" said Jahdu. "What an awful noise!"

"I don't like Thunder at all," said Yang.

"I can understand that," Jahdu told him. "Now that I'm a boy again, I don't like the cold very much either. Would you mind if I sat on the boulder and warmed myself in your light? My legs are freezing."

"I don't mind at all," said Yang.

Jahdu climbed upon the boulder. Warmth spread over the hard nature of the rock. The ice began to melt from the base of the boulder and the snow around it melted into the earth.

"Watch out, Yang!" the shade of Yin called out. "You're spreading yourself too near my field."

At once Yang retreated to the very top of the boulder. There he glowed feebly, for Yin had made him angry.

"Don't get mad at the light," Jahdu said to Yin. "He was only trying to warm my legs. I've been running a long while through this land of yours."

"I say, take care," Yin said and would say no more.

Jahdu had to pull his legs up on top of the boulder where the light of Yang was allowed to be.

"Everything has changed," Yang said softly, so Yin wouldn't hear. "Yin can choose where to lie and when to spread herself out, while I have no choice at all."

"She does act kind of mean," said Jahdu. "And here you are, barely able to cover me from head to toe."

"It's not fair," Yang said. "I don't know how much more of this I can take."

Jahdu's legs grew cramped wedged under him at the top of the boulder. Soon he had to jump up and down to rid his muscles of aches and pains.

"Woogily!" Jahdu said, getting an idea. "I'm going to have me some fun!" He leaped out into the snow and into the field where the shade of Yin lay.

Jahdu made tracks all over the shade. He took off his snowshoes and ran and leaped in circles. He screeched at the top of his voice, making the silent wasteland ring with his noise.

"Now stop it, Jahdu," said Yin. "Get back up on the boulder where you belong."

Thunder roared above Jahdu.

"Look at my pretty tracks in the snow," Jahdu yelled. He wouldn't stop until he felt like it. Yin tried covering Jahdu with shade and cold. But the fur Jahdu wore kept him warm enough. Thunder boomed and boomed again. Jahdu stuck his fingers in his ears for as long as Thunder lasted.

Suddenly Jahdu began running fast and faster. Freshly baked and strong Jahdu dust rose out of Jahdu and fell onto the shade of Yin. Softly, Yin began to sigh, for Jahdu dust had put her to sleep.

"Hey, Yang," Jahdu said, "look at this. I put Yin to sleep with my dust. I've got all of my power here in the East!"

"But Yin now has the power in this land," called Yang.

"Not anymore," said Jahdu. "Come down from that boulder and see for yourself."

Carefully, Yang allowed his light to spread down the sides of the boulder. At the base of the rock, Yang stopped to listen. Yin gently snored even though Thunder cracked and boomed.

Ice and snow melted all around the boulder. Pale light was now everywhere in the field that had once been Yin.

Jahdu jumped and leaped happily in the light. "Woogily!" he said.

"Ho!" said Yang. "I am comfortable. I am large!"

Both Jahdu and Yang saw a slow, massive movement on the northern edge of the field of snow. Quickly Yang slid back to his boulder and held himself on the very top.

Yin woke up with a start. In the land of the East, Jahdu could put things to sleep, but he couldn't make them stay asleep, even with his newly baked Jahdu dust. No, he couldn't.

"What's that coming?" Jahdu said.

"That's Yin's *friend,*" Yang said, as unkindly as he could.

Yin yawned once. Her Yin shade grew darker and then became the same shade of gray as before. "I knew she would be coming," Yin said. "I don't know why I fell asleep like that."

Yang was glad Yin didn't know Jahdu had put her to sleep. "I'm sure she didn't know her goddess was in sight," whispered Yang to Jahdu.

"Who's her goddess?" said Jahdu.

"She's nothing small," Yang said, and was silent.

The Goddess of Yin was the largest turtle in the world.

Patterned on her shell were diamond shapes the size of windows. In the center of each diamond were strange markings, like long and short lines. The great turtle's feet were as wide as rooms and wrinkles of age hung like rope from her huge, rising neck.

"Woogily!" said Jahdu. "That is some powerful-looking turtle. Where in the world do you suppose she's going?"

"To her home," said Yang, "the lake to the south, where the mists of winter hang like a shroud."

"I see," said Jahdu, staring off at the distant lake. "Look how she pulls all of the snow and ice of winter along with her. But far behind her everything is turning green. It's getting warm."

"So it seems," said Yang sadly.

"Once the turtle is in her lake, summer will come and light will be everywhere," said Jahdu.

"Wait and see," said Yang, more sadly than ever.

Jahdu thought old Yang didn't know how to have a good time. Everything was about to be all right. Winter was going to be over, and darkness, too.

The shade of Yin preened and danced around the turtle for as long as it took her to reach her water home. Then the turtle sank beneath the waters. The mists of winter parted from around the lake. Trees and flowers grew everywhere. Thunder sounded distantly and grass grew thick and long.

"My goodness, I'm getting hot," said Jahdu. He stood in the full light of Yang, which was everywhere. He pulled off most of his fur wrappings.

"Be sure to keep your clothes on top of my boulder," Yang told him.

"I don't need them," Jahdu said.

"Do as I tell you!"

Jahdu didn't like Yang ordering him about but he did as he was told. He even found his snowshoes and placed them under his clothes.

"Be sure to dig beneath the boulder," Yang told him. "Place your animal food in the hole. You'll need it when winter comes again."

"But winter is over," Jahdu said.

"It will come again! Do as I say," said Yang.

Yang's getting cranky, Jahdu thought to himself. I'd better do as he says.

So Jahdu buried his animal food beneath the boulder. Then he lay down fully in the light and got himself a deep golden tan. When he grew hot, he found a tree to lie under. Far off, he heard the sound of thunder.

"How hot it has become," said Jahdu. "I'm glad to rest in this shade." He closed his eyes, feeling peaceful. "Yin," he said, as the shade cooled him, "is that you?"

"I am here," said Yin. She laughed a cool and soft sound.

Thunder sounded nearer and Jahdu opened his eyes. Out of the heat and light of the wasteland came streaking a beautiful redbird. Like a stream of fire, it landed and walked toward Jahdu.

Jahdu smiled. "Come, my pretty bird, let me touch your feathers." The redbird had a long, lovely tail that glistened in the light of Yang. Wherever the redbird walked, shrub and glade burned with fire.

"Be careful, don't touch him!" said Yang.

The bird came close to Jahdu. Lazily, Jahdu reached out to stroke his gleaming tail.

"Woogily!" said Jahdu. "You are a firebird, but you won't burn me, will you? I like you, firebird, I surely do."

"How you doing, Jahdu?" said the redbird, with a friendly ruffle of his feathers. The redbird walked along past Jahdu. Suddenly there was a clap of thunder quite near. The redbird flapped its wings in a flash of flaming color and flew away.

"Is it going to rain?" asked Jahdu. But Yin was silent.

"Why is there thunder when there are no clouds?" Jahdu said. "I am cool—where has all the heat gone?"

Jahdu searched the sky. Clouds massed above him and over the wasteland as far as the westward edge of darkness. The clouds closed out the light.

"Ah," sighed Yin softly. "I am cool. I am large."

A tiger roared on the far side of the great she-turtle's water world.

Jahdu got to his knees in a crouch. "A tiger, here?" he said. He fitted an arrow to his bow.

"It's autumn and the white tiger comes to eat whatever there is to eat in this land," said Yin.

"A hunter tiger!" said Jahdu in a whisper. "I could use the tiger coat for winter and the tiger meat against hunger."

"Hurry to me, Jahdu!" cried Yang.

Jahdu ran for the boulder. Bow and arrow in one hand, he pulled on his fur clothing with the other. The air had turned quite cool.

Jahdu crept near the lake. He stalked Tiger and Tiger, in turn, stalked Jahdu. Thunder rolled right above Tiger's head. Tiger paused. Yin and Yang changed shade to light and light to shade. Tiger's eyes could not see so well.

After a long time of stalking Tiger, Jahdu began to wonder why the animal was always out of reach. "Even with your help I can't catch Tiger," Jahdu said to Yin and Yang, "and even though Tiger is swift and cunning he can't catch me. It would seem that we may stalk forever if we wish but never will one of us catch the other."

"Yes, it's true," said Yang.

"That's the way it is here," said Yin. "Tiger must come here and Tiger must leave again. You cannot kill him."

Jahdu walked slowly back to the boulder, since he was safe from Tiger.

"So then you do have time here in the East," Jahdu said to Yang.

"There are seasons," Yang said. "There is time for me, but not enough."

Snow fell out of the clouds as thunder sounded. A film of ice formed on the lake of the great turtle. The white tiger left the wasteland. Plants and trees quickly died. Yang was careful to cover all of Jahdu with light so that the winter would not harm him.

"How can there be just time enough for only one day of summer and autumn?" Jahdu asked.

"There has been only one day of warmth and light since the Great Change," said Yang.

"The Great Change?" said Jahdu. "Tell me about it."

Yang began to speak, slowly at first and then more quickly: "Once, long ago, the turtle belonged to both Yin and me. She walked the way along which Yin and I had power. I had all of the light of the sun and Yin kept the darkness of the moon. The turtle brought my summer in its season and Yin's winter in its time."

"But what happened?" asked Jahdu.

Before Yang could speak again, water surged and broke open the icy surface of the lake. The great turtle struggled out of the inky waters. Black mists of winter closed in the lake. Ever so slowly, the turtle came, pulling deep shadow and terrible cold of winter. Where she passed, the landscape was covered with ice and snow.

"It's simple," said Yang.

"What happened is simple?" asked Jahdu.

"Yes," said Yang. "Our turtle has grown very old. She cannot travel as quickly as she once did. And like an old, old person, she can't sit still. Once, she stayed in her water world to rest and then there would be summer. But now she enters her lake and rises quickly out of it again before her great feet grow stiff. Always she is moving, like a sleepless old one unable to stay still."

"Ah," said Jahdu, "the turtle is ancient." He bowed deeply to the massive slow-moving turtle.

"Winter has settled in," said Yang to Jahdu.

"It's a very cold-looking winter, too," said Jahdu. "Do you think the turtle will die in one of these winters?"

"I think the turtle will live an old one forever," said Yang.

"And how long is forever?" asked Jahdu.

"Almost as long as traveling in a circle," said Yang.

"Circles have no end," said Jahdu. And again he bowed to the great turtle.

"Nothing is fair in this life," said Yang sadly. "The turtle should be my goddess as she used to be."

"She should be, but she isn't. Not anymore," said Jahdu. "But don't be sad. Jahdu is here with you. Listen, we could have some fun with the turtle if you want to."

"You'd be foolish to go near her," Yang said. "She might try to eat you."

"Oh, all right, fearful cat," Jahdu said. "But be quiet awhile, will you? We have a problem. At least you do, and a friend of mine does. And if I'm going to help you and my friend, I need to think."

Yang kept quiet. Jahdu's fingers played lightly on his bowstring, making a sweet sound. Laughter was in the slant of his dark eyes but he didn't say a word. Jahdu thought and thought. When he came to the end of his thinking, he had thought of a plan.

"Watch this," Jahdu said suddenly to Yang. He fitted his sharpest arrow on his bow. He crept up behind the turtle, who had not gone far. Jahdu bowed deeply to the turtle, then took careful aim with his arrow. He pulled the arrow and string back and back, as far as they would go. Jahdu let loose both string and arrow at the same time.

"Whang!" went the bowstring as the arrow streaked across the wasteland.

62

"Ka-whuck!" went the arrow as it hit the turtle through the middle of her tail.

"Ker-purtle!" said Jahdu. "I've got me a turtle."

The Goddess of Yin spun around in a slow circle. She took a deep breath, sucking in a snow field. She blew out a roar that knocked Thunder into pieces all over the sky. It broke Yang's boulder into pebbles and lifted Jahdu off his feet in a blizzard.

Jahdu flew through the air in the worst snowstorm he'd ever seen. He had sense enough to grab hold of the last tree still left standing.

"Woogily!" he said. "This is some turtle storm, it surely is." Through the blizzard, Jahdu could see the massive shape of the turtle. The Goddess of Yin turned around and around trying to get the arrow loose from her tail. Her huge feet going in circles made a gigantic pit in the wasteland of winter. Down and down went the she-turtle in the pit. Finally, she caught hold of the arrow and tore it loose. By then, Jahdu's plan had worked.

"Yang!" shouted Jahdu. "Where are you, Yang?"

"Here," said Yang, in the tiniest voice.

Jahdu looked down and all around. At last he found Yang

in one snowflake glowing like the sun on the fur over his chest.

"I am small," cried Yang. "My boulder is gone—help me!"

"The turtle has made the biggest crater I've ever seen," said Jahdu. "And listen, Yang. That turtle's roar has torn Thunder into bits and pieces!"

Sure enough, Thunder could make noise like drums rolling. But Thunder couldn't boom anymore, like the sky falling.

"There are trees growing," said Jahdu, "and plants and grass!"

"I am comfortable!" cried Yang, for suddenly he was everywhere. "I am large!"

For six months, the turtle struggled to get out of her pit. While she labored, the wasteland bloomed with wild primrose and the sun shone brightly. But finally, in the heat of a summer's day, she worked herself free. When her massive head appeared over the edge of the pit, the weather changed to the coolness of fall.

Jahdu stayed close to Yin and Yang to make certain all would be well.

"I believe now there will be time enough," Yang said one

day to Jahdu. "Yes, the turtle who cannot stay still will have work to do."

"She'll have a hard time climbing out of that pit," said Jahdu.

"And once she's free," said Yang, "she'll not be able to change her ways. She'll go north pulling winter along with her and then she'll come back . . ."

". . . and then?" said Jahdu, leaping into the air.

"And then," said Yang, "she'll fall into the pit!"

"Woogily!" said Jahdu.

"Oh, summer will last a long time while she struggles to be free," said Yang.

Yin, who had been silent, sighed unhappily. "My goddess will never reach her water world," she said.

"But that's good!" said Yang. "Now that she is a land turtle, her huge old feet won't grow stiff."

Then Yang spoke to Jahdu: "The great goddess once again belongs to both Yin and me. The world is as it once was."

"Never again will Thunder be strong enough to hold the clouds together," Jahdu thought to say.

"Thank you, Jahdu," said Yang. "Thank you for everything."

Jahdu didn't say anything for a moment, for suddenly he felt shy. But then he spoke kindly to Yin. "I hope you won't mind sharing half of the time with Yang," he said.

"I don't care to talk about it," said Yin. "But it wasn't nice of you to make a pit for my goddess."

"Nice or not," said Jahdu, "it's done now. You'll have to get along with Yang, for he has the same power as you.

"I've got to be running along," Jahdu added.

"Come back whenever you can," Yang said very kindly. Yin said nothing at all.

"I'll do that," said Jahdu, "for here in the East I have been reborn and I might want to be born again."

Then Jahdu went running. There was light everywhere in the world. Darkness came only with the setting sun. There were people in the light, each person with his shadow. There was a giant, Trouble, searching for a new barrel. There was a crazy loon who was no longer afraid, at least, not in the daytime. He was no longer lost and he was able to see the fish he caught.

THIS IS THE END OF THE JAHDU STORY SO SWEET AND SOUR THAT MAMA LUKA TOLD ONE DAY TO LEE EDWARD.

66

"You picked the story," said Mama Luka when she had finished, "and it sure was the best old story!"

Shadow had come into Mama Luka's little room. It was suppertime, and almost time for Lee Edward to go home. Lee Edward took a while bringing himself back from the story. He shook his head as if waking from a dream.

"I wonder where Jahdu is going," he finally said.

"Jahdu is still running," Mama Luka said.

"I wonder if he will grow to be a man and stay somewhere for good," said Lee Edward.

Mama Luka looked away toward her window. "Better not to settle down," she said. "Then you won't get attached to things."

They were silent for a time. In a while Lee Edward said, very softly, "Where will you go?"

Mama Luka didn't turn from the window. "They say they will relocate me in a new home," she said. She had her hand over the letter in her pocket. When she turned to Lee Edward, her eyes were strong and bright.

"Don't you worry, Little Brother," she said. "I'll get me a nice little place on a street like this. Maybe I'll even have two rooms next time."

Lee Edward wasn't sure. "Do you think . . ." he began, "that Jahdu will come running along in your new place?"

Mama Luka laughed. "When he smells my bread a-baking, he will come shouting and running through. He will say, 'Woogily! Mama Luka, I'd love to have a taste of your bread that smells so sweet.'"

"I hope you're right," Lee Edward said. He leaned back to wait for his daddy to come for him. Mama Luka stared out her window.

Shadow in Mama Luka's room covered Lee Edward's hands. He smiled at it and whispered, "Hello, Shadow, how you doing this evening?"

But the shadow didn't answer. It just grew darker. Mama Luka rocked, making a lonely sound in her tight little room.

4.

How
Lee Edward
Went Running
Along
with Jahdu

Snow came slanting into Lee Edward's neighborhood in streams of soft flakes. People bustled by as he and his daddy walked toward home. People talked and hurried while the snow fell and Lee Edward held tight to his daddy's hand.

His daddy cradled his black lunchbox under his arm. Lee Edward wanted a black lunchbox when he grew to be a man. He looked up at his daddy and grinned.

"I bet it won't stop snowing all night," Lee Edward said.

"Going to be a big storm all right," his daddy said. "I'm glad it got going when it was time for me to quit work."

"How is it up there in a snowstorm?" Lee Edward asked. His daddy had found work on a construction gang high up in the girders of a new building.

"You have to be careful up there anytime," his daddy told him. "You don't look down any farther than your feet unless you have to."

"Are there really Indians working with you?"

"Sure," said his daddy. "They are Iroquois of the Mohawk tribe. They come from Brooklyn and they are the best men I know of for heights."

"Heights don't bother them?" Lee Edward asked.

His daddy smiled. "They work the skyscrapers like they are walking on the sidewalk," he said. "They work in riveter gangs four to a gang. A man growing old will teach high steel to his son and the son will teach it to his."

"Don't you have some Indian blood?"

His daddy laughed. "Sure, but it's not Iroquois and it's not enough to make me walk the steel beams without even looking."

"Then why do you do it?" Lee Edward wanted to know.

"I work on the rising gang, bringing the steel beams up to the riveter gangs. I'm good at it, too, and it pays for Mama Luka sitting with you."

Lee Edward told his daddy about Mama Luka's letter. They were passing Mr. Looie's Laundry a block from their home. Lee Edward's daddy was silent as snowflakes melted on his cheeks and made gray hair in his dark mustache.

"Mama Luka will get two or three nice rooms some-where," his daddy finally said. "It wouldn't surprise me if many of the old buildings came down."

"Tear down ours, too?" Lee Edward asked.

His daddy looked at him. "Ours isn't that old," he said.

Lee Edward thought awhile. Then he said, "Mama Luka might go far away from here. I'll never see her and I'll never hear the Jahdu tales." Lee Edward waited for his daddy to tell him it wouldn't be that way.

"Things don't ever stay the same" was all his daddy would say.

There were no people standing outside their building when they reached home. A wind had come up, blowing snow into their faces. There were no people anywhere around who liked the cold the way Jahdu liked it, Lee Edward thought.

Lee Edward's mama must have heard them coming up the steps. She was standing in the doorway when they reached the third floor.

"You all are snowmen," she said. "Look at you, Lee Edward, covered with snowflakes."

Lee Edward shook off the snow. He said hello softly but he didn't greet his mama with a stream of words as he usually did. He hung up his coat and sat down at the table where supper was hot and ready to eat.

"What's the matter with him?" he heard his mama say.

His daddy answered in a low voice. Lee Edward thought he heard the word "relocate."

He had to get up from the table to wash his hands. When his daddy was ready, they ate. Lee Edward was hungry but he lost his appetite. His mama asked questions about Mama Luka and even Jahdu.

"Jahdu is secret between me and Mama Luka," Lee Edward told her.

"It's nice Mama Luka's going to have a new home," his mama said.

"Can I be excused?" Lee Edward asked.

"You ate enough to feed a bluebird," his daddy told him.

"I got me something to do in my room," Lee Edward said.

"You can go," his mama said.

In his room, Lee Edward had nothing to do. He wouldn't watch his goldfish. He wouldn't play with his baseball cards. Lee Edward sat watching the snow with his face pressed against the window. He felt like he was flying upward in the snow coming down.

"It feels funny," he said to himself. "It feels like . . . shooting out of a cannon up and up." Then the outdoors turned to night.

Lee Edward was tired of flying upward anyway. He lay on the floor on the rug next to his bed. He pulled his pillow off the bed to rest his head. He lay there, just watching his fingers tap out a message on the pillow. The tapping was muffled.

What's it going to say? he wondered.

"It's going to say," Lee Edward said, tapping, "Mama Luka is going away . . . going to leave me . . . going away. . . . It doesn't say nothing."

Lee Edward lay there, his eyes half closed. The room was warm as rooms in winter can be. The steam radiator let out a long, low sigh.

Lee Edward was lying on the sidewalk in front of Mr. Looie's Laundry when Jahdu came running through.

It wasn't snowing in Lee Edward's dream. It was warm outside. As Jahdu went running by, Lee Edward called to him.

"Hey, Jahdu," he said, "wait for me."

Jahdu wouldn't stop. He kept on running. Yes, he did. And then Lee Edward was running with him. Jahdu didn't mind.

"How you doing, Little Brother?" Jahdu said.

"I'm doing fine," Lee Edward told him, "but I never did think I would meet up with you."

"You never have before," Jahdu said.

Lee Edward tried to sneak a look at Jahdu's face but he couldn't see it. They were running through the night.

"Where are we going?" Lee Edward asked.

"We'll be there soon," Jahdu said.

So Lee Edward and Jahdu went on running. Jahdu was a big high school boy or maybe older. He had his black lunchbox tucked under his arm and he was on his way to work.

"Where do you work?" Lee Edward asked him.

"We'll be there soon," Jahdu said again.

"Why are you always running?" Lee Edward wanted to know. "I'm getting tired."

Suddenly they weren't running anymore. They had

stopped in an empty place where a building was going up. Jahdu started climbing the side of the building. Lee Edward watched him go up into the clouds and stars.

"How am I going to get up there?" Lee Edward said.

"Use your wings," Jahdu told him.

Lee Edward had wings just like a bluebird. He flew up to the top of the building. But he didn't like flying. No, he didn't. He had to flap his wings so hard. When he did that, they flamed and he thought he would burn up before he got to Jahdu.

Lee Edward made it to the top. "That was scary," he said. He looked down and he saw that he was mountain high. He could see tiny lights all over the city. He could look into the room where his mama sat reading and where his daddy re-laxed in front of the TV. They were no bigger than capital letters.

"Mama," Lee Edward said. "I want to go home."

His mama looked up from her reading. "Go to sleep, Lee Edward," she said.

"I want to go home," Lee Edward said to Jahdu. Jahdu turned himself into an Indian. He was busy working on the building. He put rivets and picture windows everywhere.

There were lights focused on the building. They were blazing and they blinded Lee Edward.

"Turn off the spotlights," Lee Edward said.

"That's just Trouble's eyes a-shining," said Jahdu. "I've got him trained to help me."

"Don't let that giant catch me," Lee Edward said.

"He's not going to bother anybody. He's just sitting there in the dark, watching me," said Jahdu.

Lee Edward went to work in a big room. He spread a pile of laundry on one part of the floor. He picked up some snow and laid it out like a carpet.

"Do you think that's pretty?" he asked Jahdu about the carpet.

"I think it will melt when the sun hits it," Jahdu told him.

Lee Edward threw the carpet out of the window. He watched it fall on the tiny lights below. "So that's what makes a snowstorm," he said.

Lee Edward fell head-first out of the window. He fell into the light out of Trouble's eyes. Lee Edward didn't like falling. He could hear Loon laughing, "A-heh-heh, a-heh-heh," all the way down.

Lee Edward yelled but no sound came from his mouth.

He called for his daddy, but his voice was no louder than a whisper. Then Lee Edward was on the ground.

Jahdu was there, standing back to look at his work.

"How do you like it?" he asked Lee Edward.

"I don't like falling," Lee Edward said.

"You such a baby," Jahdu told him. "I'm talking about my building. I just finished it."

"It's a brownstone building," Lee Edward said, looking at it. He was sitting in the street. He got up and wiped slush from the seat of his pants.

"Get out of the street before you get run over," Jahdu said.

Lee Edward stepped up on the curb. "I thought you were building a skyscraper," Lee Edward said.

"I was, but I changed my mind," Jahdu told him.

"Why did you do that?" Lee Edward asked. Jahdu thought he was smart, just because he was bigger than Lee Edward.

"I didn't think a skyscraper would look right on your street," Jahdu told him.

"What?" Lee Edward said. "Hey! This new building is right next door to where I live."

"It used to be a boulder on 98th Street," Jahdu said, "but then they relocated it."

"It sure is pretty," Lee Edward said.

It was daytime. It was spring, with grass all around the building.

"Let's go in," Jahdu said. They were inside, running through rooms. Everything was newly painted.

"There's Mama Luka's rocking chair!" Lee Edward said. "And there's her jar of red licorice."

"She's got more space," Jahdu said. "She's got three full rooms of space."

"Three full rooms of Jahdu stories to tell," Lee Edward said.

"I don't know about that," Jahdu said, "she's always telling on me."

"Don't you like the Jahdu tales?" Lee Edward asked him.

"How would you like somebody always telling on you every day?" Jahdu said.

Lee Edward didn't answer him. He wouldn't tell old Jahdu that he'd never thought about it.

Mama Luka came walking in from her new kitchen. "I'm so glad you stopped by," she said. "How you doing, Jahdu? Lee Edward, I can warm up some spareribs for you, you look kind of peaked."

"You have any fresh bread for me?" Jahdu said.

"Be quiet," Lee Edward told him. "You're not supposed to ask for it." He was getting tired of Jahdu.

"Why don't you just go on home?" Lee Edward said to Jahdu.

"Yes, Jahdu," Mama Luka said, "why don't you show Lee Edward your place?"

Jahdu went out without saying good-by. Lee Edward told Mama Luka he would see her tomorrow. Then he followed Jahdu.

He and Jahdu ran down a long hall. "I'm glad she's got a place right next to my house," Lee Edward said.

"Here's my place," said Jahdu. He opened a very low door in the hallway. Inside there was one large room with just one object in it. There was a big oven right in the middle of the room. The oven door was open. Heat hit Lee Edward full in the face, knocking him down.

Jahdu laughed. "Little Brother, I got you last," he said. He dove into the oven. The door clanged shut behind him.

"You, Jahdu," Lee Edward said, "you are the worst boy!" He got to his feet and walked slowly to the oven.

"Shall I open it?" he said to himself. "Maybe Jahdu's got another trick. Maybe he will pull me inside and bake me."

"Go ahead, open it." It was Mama Luka. Lee Edward turned to her and smiled. Carefully, he opened the oven. It was dark and warm inside but now the heat had been turned off.

"Look, Mama Luka!"

"Yes, I see," said Mama Luka. In the oven there was a large loaf of bread and a sweet night-dark cake.

"I see Jahdu has run off again," Mama Luka said. "We'd better leave that bread for him when he comes back. But we can surely eat that chocolate cake."

Lee Edward and Mama Luka ate the cake. Next, Lee Edward ate spareribs and had grape juice with them. Afterward, he was still hungry. His stomach was so empty in his dream he woke up.

It took Lee Edward a while to know where he was and where he had been. He thought he was lost in Jahdu's oven. Slowly it came to him that he had crawled under his bed in his sleep. Lee Edward sighed, thankful that he wasn't a loaf of bread. He scrambled out from under his bed. Eyes wide, he looked around his room, afraid that Jahdu might be there.

Lee Edward went into the living room, where he found

his mama and daddy. His mama smiled at him but his daddy kept on watching TV.

"I'm hungry," Lee Edward said. His daddy turned to look at him.

"Have you been asleep?" his daddy asked.

"Yes," Lee Edward told him.

His mama fixed his plate and then Lee Edward brought it into the living room and sat next to his daddy. His daddy turned down the news.

"Would you like to read some after you finish eating?" his daddy said.

Lee Edward shook his head. "How long do you think it will be," Lee Edward began, "before I am grown?"

"You mean, grown as big as me?" his daddy asked him.

"I mean, grown enough to go over to Mama Luka's house wherever she goes," Lee Edward said.

His daddy had to smile. "By the time they tear down that building and move Mama Luka, you'll be grown for sure," his daddy said.

"Does it take that long to relocate somebody?" Lee Edward asked.

"By the time they get all the papers written . . ."

Lee Edward broke in, ". . . but Mama Luka already has a letter," he said.

"There are other papers," his daddy said. "There are wrecking crews to contract for. There are building crews to get and they won't usually knock down or build just one building. They will tear down many and that means a lot of paperwork."

"So I will be grown," Lee Edward said. "I'll be maybe in high school!"

"Probably the first year of junior high," his father told him.

"Is that big enough?"

"Junior-high size is big enough to travel on the subway alone," his daddy said.

Lee Edward's mama came into the room and sat down.

"Hey," Lee Edward said.

"What, hey?" his daddy said.

"You all want to hear a Jahdu tale?"

"I thought they were secret between you and Mama Luka," his mama said.

"They are, but I have me another one. One between me and Jahdu."

"Really?" his daddy said.

"Really and truly," said Lee Edward. "You want to hear it?"

"It beats television," his daddy said. He smiled at Lee Edward's mama.

"So here it comes," Lee Edward said. He rocked ever so slightly, the way Mama Luka would. "Lee Edward was lying on the sidewalk in front of Mr. Looie's, and here comes Jahdu just running through. . . ."

VIRGINIA HAMILTON was born in Yellow Springs, Ohio. After ten years in New York City, she returned with her husband and two children to Yellow Springs to live.

She is particularly proud and conscious of her heritage, and attributes these feelings to her Ohio birthplace. Her grandfather Perry was one of the many thousands of slaves who escaped from the South to Ohio, and she grew up in what had been one of the strongest stations of the Underground Railroad. The tradition and background of her childhood play an important role in all of her writing.

Miss Hamilton has written *Zeely, The House of Dies Drear, The Time-Ago Tales of Jahdu* and *The Planet of Junior Brown*. All of these books were chosen American Library Association Notable Books. *The Planet of Junior Brown* was a Newbery Honor Book.

RAY PRATHER was born in Marianna, Florida. He studied art there at Chipola Junior College and then moved to New York City, where he studied at Cooper Union.

Mr. Prather began his career as an art assistant in a New York studio. He then worked at *Look* Magazine as a designer. He has contributed illustrations to *The Nation* and *Black Enterprise*.

Mr. Prather lives in Flushing, New York.